JUDITH CASELEY

The Cousins

Greenwillow Books, New York

Watercolor paints and colored pencils
were used for the full-color art.
The text type is ITC Esprit.

Printed in Singapore by Tien Wah Press
First Edition   10 9 8 7 6 5 4 3 2 1

Library of Congress Cataloging-in-Publication Data
Caseley, Judith.
Jenny and Jessica / Judith Caseley.
p.   cm.
Summary: As first cousins grow, their parents learn how
very different Jenny and Jessica are from each other.
ISBN 0-688-08433-8   ISBN 0-688-08434-6 (lib. bdg.)
[1. Cousins — Fiction.]   I. Title.
PZ7.C2677Jen 1990
[E] — dc19   88-34903   CIP   AC

To the original first cousins,
Jenna and Jessica

J enny and Jessica were first cousins. They didn't look a bit alike.

"Night and day," said Jenny's mama. "As opposite as can be."

"Chalk and cheese," said Grandma. "You wouldn't know their mothers were sisters."

Jenny was born with lots of black hair.
"She takes after my side of the family," said
  Jenny's papa.
"Nonsense," said Grandma. "She looks just
  like my sister Bertha."

Jessica was born with one blond curl.
"Our little princess," said Jessica's papa.
"She looks just like me," said Jessica's mama.
"She's bald," said Grandma, "like her grandpa was."

Jenny crawled for the longest while.
"Will she ever walk?" asked her mama.
"Babies take their own sweet time," said the doctor.
"I'd like her to be good in gym," said Jenny's mama.
"I was," said Grandma. "She will be, too."

Jessica climbed before she could walk.

"I found her halfway up the rose trellis," said her mama.

"You can't stop watching for a minute," said Grandma.

Jenny liked to fingerpaint. Mama put on her smock and
spread newspaper on the floor.
"My little artist," said Papa, and he hung Jenny's pictures
on the refrigerator door.

Jessica liked to empty drawers and throw her toys
in the trash basket. She liked to build block houses
and knock them down.
"All that energy!" said Papa.
"I'm exhausted," said Mama.

On Jenny's third birthday, Grandma gave her a toy piano.

"Play us a tune," said Grandma.

Jenny shook her head.

Mama took Jenny's hands and helped her play a little song.

Jessica danced in time to the music.

Jenny pulled her hands away.

"No," she said, and she drew a picture instead.

"They're nothing alike," said Jenny's mama.
"Night and day," said Jessica's papa.
"Chalk and cheese," said Grandma.

On Jessica's third birthday, Grandma gave her
a big red bird that talked.
Jessica tried to make it dance instead.
It wouldn't. So Jessica put it in the closet and
shut the door.
"Oh dear," said Grandma. "They don't sell birds
that dance."

Jenny took the bird out and painted a picture of it.

"She doesn't take after me," said Papa.

"Me, either," said Mama. "I can't draw a straight line."

"She gets it from Grandpa," said Grandma. "He had
   beautiful handwriting."

When they were six, Jenny and Jessica took ballet
lessons together.
"Jessica loves it," said her mama.
"Jenny doesn't mention it," said her papa.

The next time Jenny came home from ballet class, she painted a picture.

"What a nice painting," said Mama. "What is it?"

"It's a little girl dancing," said Jenny.

"Why does she look so sad?" asked Mama.

"Her feet hurt," said Jenny.

Jenny and Jessica went to an arts-and-crafts class.
They made pictures with feathers and glitter and paint.
They made baskets and bright paper flowers.
"Isn't this fun?" said Jenny.
"No," said Jessica.

Jessica took her basket home.
  She leaped into the air and handed Mama a flower.
"How pretty," said Mama. "Do you like your class?"
  Jessica did a pirouette. "It reminds me of the dentist,"
she said.

One day Jenny and Jessica and their mamas took a
walk to the library.
They passed the dancing school. Jenny held her nose.
"Jenny is leaving dance class," said her mama.
"She likes to paint better."

They passed the community center. Jessica covered her
eyes so she wouldn't see it.

"Jessica doesn't want to go to the arts-and-crafts class
anymore," said her mama. "It reminds her of the dentist."

"They have nothing in common," said both mamas.

"Chalk and cheese," said Jenny's mama. "Night and day."

They passed the fruit market.

There was a big sign in the window:

"Try Granny Smith apples — They're one of a kind!"

"Just like me," said Jessica.

"Just like me," said Jenny.

"One of a kind!" they shouted.
  Their mothers smiled at each other.
"Smart as whips," said Jessica's mama.
"Bright as buttons," said Jenny's mama.
"Two peas in a pod!"

Then one first cousin took the other's hand,
and one sister took the other's arm,
and they all went into the library together.

E
CAS

Caseley, Judith

The cousins

DATE DUE

MAR 5			
MAR 9			
APR 1 6			
MAY 31			